MY AMERICA

Westward to Home

Joshua's Oregon Trail Diary

· Book One ·

by Patricia Hermes

Scholastic Inc. New York

St. Joseph, Missouri
1848

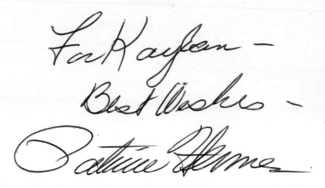

March 1, 1848

Pa is singing softly tonight! Does that mean we're going? I'm so excited I can't sleep. I lie in bed with my journal and pencil. A candle lights this page. The stars look in my window and wink at me. Do they know that I, Joshua Martin McCullough, may be sleeping under them? Do they know I might go to Oregon?

Pa's been begging Ma. He talks about free land and opportunity. Ma squinches up her eyes at him. But has she finally said yes? And what about Grampa? No. He won't go. That's why he gave me this journal. He wants me to write for him. It will be awful hard to leave my grampa.

My candle's burned to a stub. I'll write more tomorrow.

March 2

Pa still sings softly. Ma's still quiet. But Ma's always quiet. Yet something's different.

This morning, Ma was in the kitchen and Pa walked by and patted her bottom. She whispered, *"The children!"* But she smiled. I haven't seen her smile in weeks. Still, they don't say. And I don't ask. I don't want Ma to frown again.

Charlie Granger, my cousin and good friend, wants to go. But his ma, Aunt Lizzie, is like Ma. Last week, they were in our kitchen. Uncle Arthur was pestering Aunt Lizzie like a fly at a honey pot. She threw up her hands. She said, "Yes, if we all go together."

Uncle Arthur looked at Pa.

Pa nodded.

They looked at Ma.

Ma looked away.

Pa said, "What's holding us back?"

I know what's holding us back.

Ma.

March 16

Pa told me about President Polk. Our president says we should spread our country ocean to ocean. A newspaperman in New York, John O'Sullivan, wrote that it's our destiny. He called it Manifest Destiny. Now everybody says those words.

Ma says people are like parrots. Repeating words they don't even understand.

March 19

This morning Becky was coughing. Again. She coughs so hard her lips turn blue. Pa held her close. He spoke softly to Ma. I heard the words, *clean mountain air*.

Ma didn't tell him to hush. She just sighed and nodded.

Is this why she's decided to go? If she's decided.

March 20

Today Grampa came by on his horse, Daisy. Grampa has just one arm. Even so, he rides better than anyone I know. He brought me a sack of marbles. Before I could even thank him, he waved and raced out of the yard.

Grampa's my best friend. He knows my secrets. Like this: Once, I almost drowned in the pond on his farm. He pulled me out. He breathed me back to life. But only he and I know that. Only he knows that I'm still scared stiff of water. I'll miss him so bad.

Later

Guess what! Charlie said Aunt Lizzie agreed to go! But she wants her feather bed, her bureau, her rocking chair, and everything! Uncle Arthur said yes. Today, he's off to buy the biggest wagon ever.

Now Ma will say yes. She must.

She couldn't bear to let her twin sister go without her.

March 22

Yes! This morning they told me. We will go.

But Ma was still quiet. So then I said, "Ma? How come?"

Ma shrugged. She looked out the window.

I looked where she looked. Oh. We don't talk about it. But all my little baby brothers and sisters die right after they get born. The last one lived just one night. I named him Ezra. He wrapped his tiny fingers round mine. There are five gravestones out back. All that lived are me and Becky.

"Maybe in Oregon," Ma said.

I nodded. It's the most we've ever said about babies.

Nighttime

I've taken Pa's maps to my room. With my finger, I follow the trail we'll take. Mr. Robert Stuart, an explorer, laid out every step of it. In all my nine years, I've never left St. Joseph, Missouri. I've never seen anything important! I've never *done* anything important.

Maybe on the trail I'll be allowed to hunt.

Grampa had a hunting accident. That's how he lost his arm below his elbow. He was just eight years old! That's why Ma won't let me hunt. It will be different on the trail, I hope. I can't wait.

March 24

Last night, Pa gave Ma a canvas chair. He said, "You won't squat on the ground. You will sit by the campfire like a queen."

Ma laughed and shook her head.

Pa laughed, too. "Such excitement, Mrs. McCullough! And we're just beginning."

Ma said getting ready is excitement enough

to last her a lifetime. But I think Ma's happy now. She smiled even as she shook her head at Pa.

March 30

My head is spinning.

In less than one week, this has happened: We sold our house. We sold the chickens and horses. We traded the mules for oxen to pull our wagon. We've only kept our milk cow, Laurie. She'll come along. We now live in our wagon down by the Missouri River, just about a mile from our house. St. Joseph is the jumping-off place for the wagon train. There are lots of other wagons waiting by the river. An entire wagon train will go to California and Oregon.

Pa says we'll just love Oregon. We can claim a whole square mile for ourselves.

March 31

Here's what our wagon house looks like. There are hoops to hold a cover. Pa oiled the cover to make it waterproof. Inside are two chairs. There's a table and a rug. There's even a picture of Grandma on the table. It's like a tiny parlor. In the middle of it is Becky's washtub bed.

Around it are crammed barrels of dried meat and flour and coffee. There's bedding to make pallets to sleep on and spare parts for the wagon. There are Pa's rifles and Ma's wedding trunk. There's a tent for us to sleep in.

Pa's built a cupboard on the side of the wagon. It holds pots and plates and Ma's medicines. There's quinine, laudanum, and castor oil. There's also hartshorn for snakebites. Ma is scared silly of snakes. There's also a mirror on the side. Ma says she won't look in it till the trip is over. I look every day, hoping that my freckles are fading. They aren't. And my hair seems more red each day.

It's a crowded little house. But there's room for Buster, my little brown dog.

I'd just die if I had to leave Buster.

April 1

Grampa came by camp today to say good-bye. He gave me a box tied with string.

"Open it later," he said. He sounded angry, but I saw tears in his eyes. I was blinking hard myself.

When he was gone, I opened it. It was his pocket watch! It has a broad, plain face, and fat black numbers. Grampa said that when I was a baby, the ticking made me fall asleep. I looked at it a long while before I put it in my trunk.

I'm trying hard to be brave tonight.

Later

We now have our own little neighborhood.

In the next wagon are Aunt Lizzie, Uncle Arthur, Charlie, and little Rachel. Rachel is four and a best friend to Becky.

Next wagon are the Wests with their son, Adam. Adam is quiet. I think he's afraid of his pa. Nobody likes Mr. West very much. He's loudmouthed. But we like Mrs. West.

Then there are Mr. and Mrs. Gibbons from our church. They call their babies the January, February, and March babies. The oldest, January, is a boy. He's two. February is a girl. She's one year old. And March is so new she can't hold her head up yet. Everyone likes them. Aunt Lizzie says they act as if they were newlyweds. But Ma said, "With three babies?"

Then there are Mr. and Mrs. Allison. They're fat and they laugh at everything. They have no children, just a dog. Its name is Adorable. Honest. I didn't even laugh when I heard it. Adorable wears a hair ribbon and sits on Mr. Allison's lap all day long.

In another wagon are the Douglas sisters, Miss Emmaline and Miss Elizabeth. They're single ladies from Ohio. Everyone wonders why they're traveling alone. They're nice enough, but a bit standoffish.

Then, there are the Druckers. There are about twenty of them traveling together in three wagons. In one wagon, there's a mama, a papa, a little girl named Sarah, and a girl my age called Bobbi. She's real lively. The Druckers come all the way from Kentucky.

Lastly, there are Mr. and Mrs. Meaney. I am *not* making up that name. Mrs. Meaney is as nasty as her name. I've known her for a week and I've yet to see her smile.

And there are lots of other wagons, maybe

a hundred altogether, strung out along the river.

We're a mixed group, but Pa says we will get along well.

I'm not so sure about the Meaneys.

April 2

Today the men chose a guide for our train. His name is Cousin Daniel, but he's not cousin to anyone we know. Pa voted for him because he's led other wagon trains. Cousin Daniel warned us about Indian raids and snakes and hailstorms. He said this trail isn't for cowards.

Then he took off his boots and showed us his feet. One foot has no toes at all! He said he wore his toes right off with walking all the way to Oregon!

Charlie whispered to me, "Is it true, you think?"

"Nah," I said back.

Cousin Daniel heard and he grinned at me. "You're right, boy," he said. "I'll tell you the real truth. I was sleeping one night, and a snake crawled up and bit them right off of me."

Later, Pa said he really lost his toes to frostbite.

Pa also said not to worry. Cousin Daniel is full of bluster. But he will be a good guide.

April 3

We're waiting for the grass to green up. Cousin Daniel says that feed for animals is hard to come by. On the trail, God gives us grass. He's right. We could never carry enough feed for the animals.

Who would have thought that our whole trip must wait on grass!

April 5

Still waiting. Everyone's restless, even the animals.

To pass the time, Pa did some sums in a book. He added up the cost of all the supplies and animals and wagons camped here. It came to one hundred thirty thousand dollars!

I've never seen even three dollars at one time.

I know Ma and Pa have one hundred eighty dollars for our trip.

April 6

Pa worries that we're waiting too long. If we delay, we won't make it to Oregon before winter. It's going to take us six whole months.

People tell about one wagon train, the

Donner train going to California. They got lost in the mountains and had to stop for the winter. Some people froze to death and some starved to death. To survive, they cooked and ate their dog, and worse.

Charlie grinned at Buster. He said, "I bet dogs taste good."

I held Buster close. I said, "Don't listen, Buster. He's just trying to scare you."

April 7

Grampa is coming. He raced into camp yesterday on Daisy! He has just his saddlebags and some gold. He'll buy what he needs at the supply posts. He said I should write in my journal anyway. "Someone needs to record such madness," he said. Then he muttered about what mischief I could get into without him.

I know the truth: He would miss me.

April 8

Last night Grampa slept under the wagon with me. We talked about Oregon and buffalo and Indians. And then, so odd! Grampa talked about Grandma. He hardly ever does that. She died when I was just a baby so I don't remember her. He said it was hard to leave her grave. I felt a kind of lump in my throat when he said that. I never before thought that he might be lonesome.

We talked until the whole camp was dark and just some embers glowed in our fire. We fell asleep talking.

I'm real glad that Grampa is here.

April 10

Today our wagons moved out! There must be one hundred wagons, strung out along the trail. Some are fancy. Some are plain. Some are in-between, like ours. Some have words painted on them. Many say: OREGON OR BUST! Some say: MANIFEST DESTINY.

Pa wanted to paint ours, too. "What shall it be?" he asked Ma. "GOING HOME"?

Ma told him to wait till we got to Oregon. Then we'll see if it's home or not.

April 13

We've ridden and walked for days. And yes, the grass is green. But I can hardly see it! The dust is so thick I choke. And it smells — like hot animals and animal droppings. Charlie and I tied handkerchiefs over our faces.

I feel sad for the animals. Little brown Buster is gray with dust. When we stopped tonight, Pa sent me to care for Laurie, our cow. Her eyes were caked shut with sand.

Charlie helped me wipe her clean. When he took off his handkerchief, I laughed. He was brown around his eyes and forehead and white under his handkerchief. I said he looked like a raccoon. He said I did, too.

April 14

This is our routine. We wake before sunrise to Cousin Daniel blowing his bugle. The men round up the cattle and hitch up the oxen. We roll up our pallets. The women make breakfast of dried meat and bread and coffee and we eat. The women and girls use sand to clean the plates and then rinse them in water. We reload the wagons. And off we go — twenty miles every day.

Women sit in the wagons and knit. I don't know how they do it, with the way the wagons sway. The men and children walk, all but the tiny ones. Mr. and Mrs. Allison and Adorable always ride. They're old and fat and they pant just walking from wagon to wagon to visit at night. Even Adorable gets out of breath from walking.

April 24

We have scouts who ride ahead. They look for Indians and wolves, and for a safe place to stop at night.

When we stop, we make circles of wagons. The front tongue of one wagon gets locked to the rear of another. We make several big circles. There's an open space left, like a horseshoe. The animals are tethered and guards are set to watch. The children play inside the horseshoe.

Becky's one of the youngest. Yet she bosses all the other children. Today, I heard her tell little January, "You can be the daddy. Rachel is our baby."

Rachel said she didn't want to be the baby. So Becky went to Mrs. Gibbons. She asked if she could borrow the March baby.

Mrs. Gibbons laughed but she said no.

April 27

At night, over the fires and the smell of coffee and sizzling meat, the women gossip.

A lot of the talk is about the Douglas sisters.

Mrs. Gibbons wondered why single women would be on the trail alone. Aunt Lizzie said she heard they're planning to homestead on their own.

I said, "A woman could never do that."

Ma said, "Don't be too sure of that, young man!"

April 28

Not even three weeks out, and something awful happened already. Our wagon was going along a rocky bluff. On the far side, the wagons began to rush down. Even with brakes dragging them, they fairly flew. The Allisons' wagon bounced against another. Mr. Allison and Adorable toppled off. The front wheels ran over Mr. Allison. Before we could stop, the back wheels ran over him. And they ran over Adorable. Mr. Allison screamed something awful. And then, it was more awful. Because he stopped screaming.

I can't write more.

Later

Mr. Allison's leg got cut off. He died right there. Adorable got all mushed and dead.

Mrs. Allison stared. And then she said very sadly, "*Well.*" Fat tears ran down her face. She took the reins of her oxen. The men helped her turn her wagon toward home. She drove off. She didn't wait to see Mr. Allison put in the ground. We buried him, his leg, and Adorable, too. We ran wagons over the grave. That's so the Indians won't find it and dig it up. Cousin Daniel says they dig up graves to get at the clothes. They especially like the buttons.

Tonight Cousin Daniel said that Mr. Allison's just the first to go. There will be more, he said.

Ma told him to shut his mouth. My ma! She actually said those words. Sometimes I think Ma should have been born a man.

April 30

Last night the Drucker family moved their wagon up near ours, where the Allisons' wagon used to be. After supper, when the sky was blue-black, and the stars were winking, the men took out dulcimers. They call them hog fiddles. They began to play and the women began to dance. Bobbi and her little sister Sarah climbed up on the tail of the wagon. They did a regular barn dance, their feet flying. Aunt Lizzie grabbed Ma's hands. But Ma pulled back.

Pa clapped his hands and began to sing.

I wished I dared join in. But I thought I might look foolish.

May 1

Mrs. Meaney has a wide, turned-up nose and pointy ears. She looks just like a pig. She's as mean as a pig, too. Every morning, Mr. Meaney carries her outside and puts her in a chair. She sits there knitting and complaining. She complains how hard the chair is. "Oh, I am comfortless!" she says. She says it loud. I know she has her eye on Ma's chair.

May 2

Sure enough. Last night, Ma brought over her very own chair — the canvas one Pa bought her! Ma said Mrs. Meaney could use it for the rest of the trip.

And do you know something? Mrs. Meaney never even said thank you. She just said, "I can sure use it, dearie."

I knew she was a pig.

May 5

Tonight Mrs. Meaney was knitting and complaining like usual. Then I saw her coax Buster to her. She held out a bit of cake. When he got close, she popped the cake in her own mouth.

Buster yapped at her.

She screamed, "Vicious dog!"

Now Ma says I have to keep Buster tied up in camp so he won't bother her. If I were Buster, I wouldn't yap at her. I'd bite her ankles. Except they're probably poison.

May 7

There's a family here from Ohio named the Hulls. They've been in the rear, but last night they moved up near us and their friends, the

Druckers. The Hulls have lots of children in all sizes.

One boy is named Frederick. He's ten years old, but as big as a bull. Today he walked with Charlie and Adam and me. Secretly, Charlie and I named him Me Too. Everything we do, he does. I kick a stone, he kicks a stone. I pick up a stick, he picks up a stick. Tonight he saw me writing in my journal. I believe somehow he'll get himself a journal.

His mother's health is frail. She lies in the wagon, even on the trail. Mrs. Drucker says that Mrs. Hull will have another baby soon. Imagine! Another baby. I think they have a dozen already.

May 10

Hot. Hot. Hot.

May 17

Cousin Daniel says we've crossed into Nebraska and will be at Fort Kearney soon. There we'll get supplies. Ma needs more medicines. The Epsom salts have been used up, soaking sore feet.

Grampa needs new shoes made for Daisy. He says they'll cost three dollars each! And he wants a new gun.

Guess what Mrs. Meaney needs? A feather bed and a pillow — of course! Mr. Meaney just says, "Yes, dear heart."

I sometimes wish it was Mrs. Meaney who fell off the wagon and got run over. Then I ask God for forgiveness.

Fort Kearney

Mrs. Hull's baby was born this morning. He's been named Kearney for the fort. He's the ugliest baby I've ever seen. He hasn't stopped wailing since he got born. Maybe he saw himself in our mirror. He's baby number fifteen for them!

Imagine!

Fort Kearney, nighttime

I have to tell about the fort. There are lots of soldiers. There's a smithy and a store and supplies. The walls and houses are made of sod. It doesn't look much like a fort to me. But when we camped here, I saw my first Indian! Actually, I saw many, many Indians. They're everywhere. They're not wild. Our men often smoke pipes with them. Our women make them tea.

But Cousin Daniel doesn't trust them. He says, "Don't turn your back, or they'll put an arrow in it."

Sometimes I think I hate Cousin Daniel.

Next morning

We left the fort early. Across the river we saw a Mormon wagon train. Some of the Mormon men waved to us. We children waved back. The Mormons had bad things happen to them. Their leader, Joseph Smith, was killed and Grampa said it was only because people didn't like his beliefs.

They're going to find a new home in Utah.

Pa told me that Mormon men can have lots of wives. He then added, "Heaven forbid. One is enough!"

That's because Ma is cross with everything now. There were so many mosquitoes and tadpoles in her cup of water yesterday that she tossed it out. "It's alive!" she said. "To think one would drink a cupful of bugs."

May 23

Bobbi walks with Charlie and Adam and Me Too and me. Her mama doesn't mind her walking with the boys. But some of the mamas won't let their girls do that. Mrs. Meaney is always making sharp comments about Bobbi.

Bobbi says Mrs. Meaney reminds her of the mosquitoes. They bite and nip at you, and you always want to slap them.

I think I'll like Bobbi just fine.

May 26

We were setting up camp tonight. Suddenly the sky turned black. The wind whipped sand around us and the oxen lowered their heads. We tried to turn our backs, but sand was everywhere. Even my mouth got full of it.

And then the rain just poured down. I saw Adam run to his pa. And his pa pushed him away!

Charlie and I huddled under the wagon. But we were still soaked through. Ma says not to worry, the weather will dry out soon.

It can't be soon enough for me.

May 27

I'm still wet. And shivering. And it's still raining. My book is soaked through. I don't dare turn a page for fear it will tear. I'll write some more when the sun comes out.

May 29

The sun will never come out. Three days and it's still raining. Water runs down my neck. My plate fills with water when we eat. My shoes squish water. I sleep in mud. Today I saw a snake swimming alongside me. Ma yelled to watch out. Even Pa seems fed up tonight. He snapped at Becky when she soiled herself. He told Ma that Becky was too big to do that, and Becky cried.

When I went to comfort her, Pa and Ma both glared at me.

I took Becky outside. We played in the mud under the wagon. Why not? We were soaked through anyway.

Morning, May 30

The sun came up so bright this morning, I could yell for happiness. Everyone stood around, soaking it up. Ma and Aunt Lizzie laid out bedding to dry. Pa smiled and put a hand on my head. I know he's sorry for being snappish.

Only Grampa seems grumpy this morning. I think his arm aches when it's wet.

May 31

Buster disappeared so I walked back, looking for him. I walked. And looked. And walked. And walked. Suddenly it was too quiet. I looked around. I couldn't hear the wagons. I couldn't see the dust.

I stood still, my heart thumping hard.

Was I lost?

And then — there was Buster! He was sitting on a small rise, making pitiful little sounds. And, oh! His paws were split and bloody.

I snatched him up and hugged him and he licked my face. I climbed the little rise and stood on tiptoe, looking around. Nothing. No dust. Nothing but grasses as tall as my head. And silence.

I was lost. *Lost.*

I looked at the sky. The sun was low. What should I do? I was already so thirsty. But which way to go? My heart was thundering. West. We'd been heading west. I took a deep breath. I held Buster close and headed into the setting sun and prayed.

I walked for a long, long time. The sun set and it turned black. It was so black I couldn't see my own feet and I kept stumbling. How long had I been gone? Did anyone even know I was missing?

I don't think I've ever been so scared. Buster got heavy, but I couldn't put him down because he might run off into the dark. Please, God, please, I prayed. Let me find them. Let *them* find *me*. But what if they never found me? You could die of thirst in just one day, I knew that. And the buzzards would come. And wolves.

No, don't think that, I told myself. Don't think. And then, just as the stars winked overhead, I heard it — hoofbeats.

"Here!" I yelled. "I'm here."

The hoofbeats came closer. But what if it was Indians? I didn't care. "I'm here!" I yelled again.

And Grampa came thundering up on Daisy.

June 2

Today I walked alongside my friends again. I promised Ma I wouldn't leave them, not even for a second. We crossed a wide, sandy place. Ahead of us, we could see mountains looming. The wind blew something fierce, and I used axle grease to soothe my lips. But they're so dry, they bleed. I covered my head with my shirt. But then the sun beat on my shoulders. It seems there's no way out of the sun and heat. Except when it rains. And then there's no way out of the rain.

Adam was quiet today so I asked what he was thinking. He said he was praying. I wondered if he prayed for me the day I was lost.

I wish I was good like him. All I do is complain.

Ash Hollow

All of our spirits are raised again. The scouts rode ahead and found this fine spot. A breeze blows and there's a fresh stream. The mountains are all about, and above us is Chimney Rock. It's split at the top, as though by a lightning bolt.

I took Becky to show her. She tilted her little head back and looked up, smiling. I realized something then — at home, Becky used to cough and cough, especially at night. Now she rarely coughs, even with all the dust. Around us stars were winking and the mountain was turning purple. I whispered to God a little thank-you prayer.

Suddenly I saw something. It wasn't just me and Becky there. Bobbi was there, too. She smiled at me.

I sort of smiled back. I wanted to say something, but couldn't think what.

I wish now I had said something clever.

Fort Laramie, June 10

This fort is not at all like Fort Kearney. This one has tall walls and a big courtyard. And Indians everywhere. Some were even sleeping on top of the walls.

Our men and women went poking around inside the fort. We children were told to stay outside. But Charlie and Bobbi and I sneaked in. We found rooms, like bedrooms. There were buffalo skins spread on the floors for beds. There were decorations on the walls. And in one room there was a scalp hanging from the wall! Sometimes some Indians kill people and keep their scalps as trophies. This scalp had hair on it about three feet long.

Charlie dared Bobbi and me to touch it.

I touched the hair. Bobbi touched the scalp part.

We all acted like we weren't afraid. But I think we were. I keep thinking about whose head it was.

June 11

The temperature on our thermometer today said one hundred ten degrees.

June 12

Rachel and Becky climb in my lap for stories at night. Becky keeps talking about buffalo. She says it like this: *buffo*. She even calls Laurie, our cow with the twisted horn, a buffo.

Tonight, Rachel gave me a wildflower. Very seriously, she said, *"I like you."*

June 13

Folks are suddenly very ill. Ma scurries from wagon to wagon with medicines. But two of our party died today, and we passed six graves from an earlier wagon train.

Folks get sick in the morning and are dead by sundown. We can't stop to nurse them. We barely stop long enough to bury them. Ma's afraid it's an outbreak of cholera.

June 14

So many more folks are ill.

Farther back in our train, there's a family of

six. Both the ma and pa died today. That leaves four orphans.

Folks offered to take one or two children. But the eldest girl is twelve. She won't part with any of the little ones. She says she'll be the mother now.

Imagine.

June 15

Two babies died last night! One was the tiny Gibbons baby, Baby March. The other was the new Hull baby, little Kearney. Pa and Grampa dug their grave this morning. We buried both babies together. At first, Mrs. Gibbons wouldn't give up her baby. Pa had to take it from her arms.

I saw Pa wipe his face in his handkerchief. I wonder if he was crying.

June 17

The bugle woke us before the sun was up. It was Cousin Daniel, shouting orders. The river's rising and we must cross it.

We scrambled things together. Becky sat in the wagon with Ma. Aunt Lizzie and Rachel sat in theirs. Pa took the reins of the oxen on one side. I was on the other side. Men on horseback swam into the river to guide the wagons. My heart was thundering.

Within minutes, the oxen were swimming. But they began swimming downstream! Pa yelled. Cousin Daniel yelled. Men began shooting off their rifles. I saw Bobbi pick up a rifle and begin shooting. I didn't know what to do.

Suddenly Grampa was in the water beside me on his horse. He yelled at me to guide Daisy. Then, with just his one arm, he grabbed the reins of the oxen. In just a minute or two, the oxen turned and swam across.

I felt ashamed. Was it my fault the oxen swam downriver? Wasn't I strong enough? Did they feel how scared I was?

Later

Pa says it wasn't my fault. Oxen have a mind of their own, he said. At least our wagon stayed upright. Two others overturned. One of the overturned wagons belonged to the Douglas sisters.

All their things got dumped out. A gown got all swollen up in the water and floated away.

Bobbi stood beside me. "Look!" she whispered, pointing with her rifle. "It looks like a dead lady."

The floating lady was followed by barrels of flour and everything. Miss Emmaline's face got as white as snow. Grampa told her not to fret. We'll all help out. We will. But now they have nothing!

Night

Tonight, folks brought things to the Douglases' wagon. Aunt Lizzie brought a petticoat. Mrs. Drucker brought a bonnet. Ma brought a fry pan. She said she had two and one wouldn't be missed. Mr. Gibbons gave them a whole barrel of flour. He said maybe they'd bake some fine things for him. Mrs. Gibbons usually doesn't mind what folks say — that she doesn't know much about cooking. Tonight, she didn't even smile. She grieves so for her March baby.

Mrs. West is timid, much afraid of her husband. It seems more and more clear that he's a bully. She waited until he'd gone to bed down the animals. Then she tiptoed over to the Douglas wagon. She handed Miss Emmaline a brand-new apron. She whispered that it hadn't even been worn yet. She was saving it to wear in Oregon.

It was nice to see everyone helping.

June 18

No one has died in two days. The sickness seems to have run its course. But Cousin Daniel says it will come back.

I waited for Ma to tell him to shut up. She just turned away.

June 20

Today when we were walking, Bobbi and I played "I Spy." Once, Bobbi said, "I spy a wagon."

We both burst out laughing.

Only thing is: I see Me Too and Adam and Charlie smirking at me. I know they think Bobbi is sweet on me. She's not.

She's just my friend.

June 21

Today, Bobbi and I were walking together. The others fell behind.

Suddenly I heard a sound. I looked around. Charlie and Adam and Me Too had crept up on us. Adam and Charlie were grinning at me from behind their hands. And Me Too was making kissy sounds right out loud.

I hate that! I hate them. I scooped up a handful of dung to throw at them. But they ducked away.

Bobbi just shrugged.

But then she went off to her wagon. I went and rode with Grampa a while.

In camp

Still no buffalo. But today we saw buffalo chips and footprints. Cousin Daniel warned: Where there are buffalo, there are Indians.

Bobbi said not to worry. The Indians will be friendly.

Charlie asked her how she knew that. He said it in a kind of mean voice.

She said, "I just know. The Pawnee and the Arapaho have been real friendly. The Lakota seem friendly. Most Indians are friendly."

When she went to her wagon, Charlie said she's a big know-it-all.

June 22

I woke up early. The camp was still asleep. Stars shone but the sky was just beginning to lighten. I saw something white hanging from Charlie's wagon. I crept over to see. My heart caught in my throat. It was Rachel. She was hanging upside down. Her nightdress was caught in the axle of the wagon. She was just hanging there.

"Rachel?" I said.

I tried to lift her up. I couldn't. She was stuck. She didn't answer. But her eyes were open.

"Rachel!" I said it loud. Aunt Lizzie stuck her head out of the wagon. She screamed.

Uncle Arthur and Pa scrambled out from beneath the wagons. Pa pulled his knife from his belt. He cut Rachel's gown loose. But it was too late. Rachel was dead.

Everyone is crying.

My throat is so tight I think I will choke.

Later

Rachel got hung by the sash of her nightdress. We wonder where she was going in the night. Aunt Lizzie cries and cries. Ma acts like she has been struck dumb. Charlie doesn't speak. Pa and Uncle Arthur look stunned.

Grampa and I went off to the creek. Grampa put tobacco in his pipe.

We sat side by side. I wanted him to say something to make it better. But he didn't say anything at all.

Later still

Cousin Daniel shouts at us to move out. But Aunt Lizzie won't move until there's a decent grave for Rachel. The men dug a deep hole. Aunt Lizzie shook her head. She said it wasn't deep enough. The wolves would dig it up.

She climbed in the grave herself and began to dig.

Uncle Arthur took the shovel from her. He said he'd see the grave went six feet down. He promised.

June 23

We just go on. Charlie doesn't speak much. Ma and Pa are silent, too. They hug Becky to them. I know they're thinking of Rachel. My heart hurts.

Night

Tonight, Aunt Lizzie brought Rachel's things to Ma. There was a bonnet, a little dress, some underthings. She said she wouldn't be needing them now. Maybe Becky could use them.

She stood there before Ma, the baby clothes in her hands. Ma just looked at her. Then she reached for Aunt Lizzie. They hugged. And then the two of them cried and cried.

I hope Ma never puts those clothes on Becky.

June 24

Something strange.

Today, Charlie and Bobbi and I went to collect buffalo chips. Some are nasty, wet and slimy. But the dry ones are good for the fires. Bobbi is the only girl who will help collect them. Charlie picked up a buffalo chip. Suddenly he threw it at me. He picked up another. He threw that. At first I was surprised. Then it was a game. I threw one. He threw one. I threw one.

Bobbi began to throw them.

But then I saw — Charlie was crying. Tears just ran down his face. Had I hit him?

"Did I hurt you?" I asked.

He shook his head and kept right on crying. I thought I knew why he cried.

Then, I'm kind of ashamed of this. I looked to see if Bobbi was watching. She wasn't. She was staring at the ground. So I put my arm around Charlie's shoulder.

He seems a bit more cheerful tonight.

June 25

Buffalo! They're way out across the prairie. They're no more than small black dots. When we camped tonight, men went from wagon to wagon, taking votes. Should we stop to hunt?

Mrs. Meaney looked up from her knitting. "No!" she shouted. But women have no say in these matters. Cousin Daniel said the men have buffalo fever. But, though he doesn't want to waste a day, he agreed. For all the men voted yes. Everybody wants fresh meat after all the dried meat we've been eating.

So early tomorrow morning, the men will hunt.

Pa won't go. Some men have to stay to guard the wagons. I begged Grampa to let me join the hunt. He squinted up his eyes at me. He said, "We'll see."

That usually means no.

June 26

I'm so tired I can hardly hold this pencil. But I must write this: Today I went on the buffalo hunt. I rode with Grampa, ahead of him on his saddle. The sun wasn't up yet. There were many men in our party. Soon, though, Grampa and I were far ahead. There, on the plains ahead, were buffalo. Hundreds of them. They are so, so big! Their heads are as big around as wagon hoops, it seems. They looked at us, not at all afraid. When we got close, we stopped. Softly, Grampa and I slid down and hobbled Daisy.

Grampa took the cover off his rifle. He squinted through it. I could see him aim for a huge bull that looked our way.

Grampa turned. He handed me the gun. He said, "Your shot, son! Line it up in your sights. Right through the lungs."

I could hardly believe it. Me? Me?

He nodded.

I felt my heart thundering. I looked through the sights. I let off a shot and then another.

I, Joshua Martin McCullough, have killed a buffalo.

Later

The rest of the day was hard. We skinned the buffalo and cut it into steaks. There was blood and guts everywhere. It almost made me dizzy. Cousin Daniel cut some of the meat into thin sheets for drying. The meat will be a good change to our dull diet. Some nights I dream of food. I especially dream of eggs.

June 27

Except for yesterday and the hunting, I hardly see Grampa anymore. He spends all his time riding beside the Misses Emmaline and Elizabeth. Ma sniffed when I told her. She said that Grampa had so little sense, he might end up married again.

Imagine. The sisters are younger than Ma even.

June 28

Cousin Daniel called it a hill. It was more like a mountain. We had to unload our wagons and haul things up by ropes and chains. Even our wagons needed to be hauled by chains.

Things slid out, and people slid down. Two tiny Hull girls tried to jump over the front of their wagon. Their skirts got caught up on the yokes. They almost got run over. Grampa grabbed one. Cousin Daniel got the other.

And do you know — both little girls laughed!

Grampa paddled the bottom of the girl he held, and she howled.

But I'm happy. We don't have to bury two more children tonight.

Nighttime

Something bad. Bobbi followed me when I went to hobble the horses. She was chattering in that way she has, talking about the two little Hull girls almost falling under the wagon wheels. I wasn't saying much.

Suddenly, she said, "How come you won't talk to me anymore?"

I said, "I talk to you." But I didn't look at her.

She said, "Not like you used to."

I shrugged.

She made this huffy noise through her nose. "You're scared of what those dumb boys say?"

"They're not dumb!" I said.

"They make kissy sounds," she said.

"So?" I said.

"So you're scared of them," she said.

"Am not!" I said.

"You're a chicken!" she said. "That's what." Then she made this "Bawk, bawk!" sound at me. She ran away, her skirts twisting around her ankles. But I thought she was crying.

Tonight, I feel like such a — chicken.

Later

After supper, I asked Ma if I could take Becky to the Druckers' wagon. I said maybe she'd like to play with Bobbi's sister, Sarah. I know she must miss Rachel. I also thought I could talk to Bobbi.

Ma shook her head no. She hasn't let Becky out of her sight since Rachel's accident.

In camp, I see Mrs. Hull and Mrs. Gibbons and Aunt Lizzie. Three mamas. Three dead babies.

It must be hard to be a mama.

June 30

Tomorrow we have to ford a river that's running high. We'll turn the oxen free and float the wagons across. Tonight we spent hours adding more caulk to the wagon box so it will float.

Pa says this time my job will be to stay in the wagon with Ma and Becky. I'll try to shift our belongings if the wagon tilts.

Yay! I won't have to get in the water!

July 1

I'm so tired when we stop each day. We're all so tired. Even the oxen are exhausted and weak from the loads. Today Cousin Daniel rode back along the trail. He said each wagon has to leave some heavy things behind.

Uncle Arthur put his bureau and Aunt Lizzie's rocking chair out along the trail. Ma left her wedding trunk and framed pictures. Mrs. Gibbons left a baby cradle. I saw it rock in the wind, all empty and sad.

Mrs. Meaney said she wouldn't leave a single thing. "I'm already as poor as a snake!" she cried.

Cousin Daniel started to say something. Then he seemed to change his mind.

I wish he'd left Mrs. Meaney behind. She *is* a snake.

July 2

Aunt Lizzie is ill. For weeks now, she vomits in the mornings. She spends much of her day lying inside the wagon. I wonder if Rachel's death has made her ill.

I worry that she'll die. Then what will Charlie do?

Afternoon

We were making camp. Out across the prairie, we saw figures coming fast. Indians on horseback.

Suddenly Cousin Daniel dug in his pack. He came out with the most amazing thing — a military jacket. He put it on. Then he picked up his rifle.

Everyone got still and quiet. The Indians came thundering up to us. There must have been a hundred of them. They were big and dark, and some had painted faces. Their heads were shaved, but for tufts of hair on top. Their horses snorted and stamped.

Cousin Daniel said how do. The Indians said how do.

One brave stared at Grampa for a long time. Then he offered his daughter in trade for Daisy!

Grampa said no.

Cousin Daniel gave them some tobacco and beads. They gave Cousin Daniel a buffalo skin. Then they rode off.

Cousin Daniel says they may come back later for Grampa's horse. We'll set extra guards to watch tonight.

Night

I found out why Cousin Daniel put on his military jacket. Indians, he said, respect the military. They've been warned not to attack. If they do, their nation will be wiped out.

I thought that a very terrible thing to say to any man.

July 3

More Indians today. Our wagon was in the front of the line. That's because we change places, so that not everyone gets all the dust from the front wagons. We came over a rise, and there was an entire village. There were men and women and children and dogs.

I held Buster close.

The Indians didn't seem interested in us. But I kept looking at them. I thought about what Cousin Daniel said yesterday about wiping out the Indian nation. It must be hard to be an Indian.

July 4

For some reason, everyone seems happy tonight. After supper, music and dancing began again.

This time, some men joined in with the women. And then Charlie poked me. I stared. Grampa! My grampa! He was dancing with one of the sisters. It was Miss Emmaline.

Later I heard Ma tell Pa that Grampa was making a fool of himself. Pa just smiled. I turned away from Ma. Because I was smiling, too.

July 5

We're moving even slower now. Cousin Daniel pushes us. We were supposed to reach Independence Rock by yesterday, July fourth, Independence Day. So we're behind schedule, but not by much. It's awfully hot. It's as if all the days of July and August got all rolled up in one.

Sweetwater River

Another river crossing. Cousin Daniel says we'll cross it several more times. When Mr. Stuart made this trail, couldn't he make it straight? I bet he wasn't scared of water. If he had been, he'd never have done it this way.

Independence Rock, July 6

We are too tired to celebrate.

South Pass

We've crossed the Continental Divide. On one side, the rivers flow east to the Atlantic.

On the other side, the rivers flow west to the Pacific. Pa tells me that's why it is called the divide.

I should feel excited. I just feel tired.

Ice Slough

We've found ice. Yes. Truly! Here, in winter, the river backs up and fills up the land. It freezes deep down. You can cut down into it and find ice! I cut deep and came up with an ice chunk and gave it to Bobbi. She thanked me, but her voice was as cold as the ice. She didn't even look at me.

I threw an ice chunk at Charlie. It missed and almost hit Mrs. Meaney. She ducked under that ugly blue thing she is knitting. And she howled like a wolf.

I said, "I'm sorry, Mrs. Meaney."

But I wasn't sorry. I'm not sorry.

Next day

We stopped early today.

Charlie and Adam and Me Too and I were sent to pick berries. We were careful to pick only the ones we knew to be blackberries. Me Too stuffed his mouth full. He ate more berries than he picked. No wonder he's so fat.

Night

Me Too is very sick tonight.

Ma thinks he ate black nightshade berries. She brought laudanum to the Hulls' wagon. She thinks he might not live.

July 15

This morning rifle shots awakened us. I jumped so hard I bumped my head on the wagon.

Pa rushed out from under the wagon.

Mrs. Meaney began wailing, "Indians, Indians!"

But there were no Indians. Cousin Daniel said he just needed a change from the bugle.

Nobody thought it was funny.

Later

A wolf's been following our train. A pack of them stands off on the horizon. At night we see them outlined against the sky. But one seems brazen. He follows us in broad daylight. Ma says he spooks her. It is as though he's waiting for someone to die and get buried so he can dig the poor soul up. I wonder if it will be Me Too. I don't like him, but I don't want him to die.

Nighttime

Tonight when we made camp, Pa set out with his rifle. He said he'd see to that wolf but good, bothering and worrying Ma the way it did.

But guess what? As soon as the wolf saw the rifle, he took off. Pa hadn't even let off a shot. And now we hear the wolf in the distance. *How ooh*, he calls, *how ooh*. I would swear that he's laughing.

July 16

Me Too is a little better. At least, he's not dead.

July 18

Five of our men are missing. They're the scouts who go ahead. They haven't come back to our wagon train tonight. We're afraid that something has happened to them.

July 19

The five are still missing. One of them is Mr. Gibbons, the father of the January, February, and March babies. Mrs. Gibbons looks as though she has seen a ghost.

She doesn't even speak tonight.

July 21

Mrs. Gibbons wept all night. I could hear her in her wagon. Ma took Becky and went to stay with her. Pa said the men were found. Killed by arrows.

Fort Hall, August 3

We are at the fort! At last. For the past weeks, we've been very afraid, knowing that our men have been killed.

But here there are Indians all about, just as at the other forts. And they are friendly. One Indian gave Pa a buffalo skin — just tossed it to him. And not for any reason. Pa went to our wagon and brought back some tobacco. He gave it to the Indian man.

That bully, Mr. West, he told Pa he had no business exchanging gifts with Indians. Pa just ignored him. And then Pa and the Indian sat down and smoked their pipes together.

It is confusing. But I do believe this: Indians are a lot like the rest of us. Some are good. And some are not.

Fort Hall, still

Here some families will leave us. One part of the trail branches north to Oregon. The other goes south to California.

The three Drucker wagons gather round. They had planned to go to California, but now some say Oregon. At night, they squabble among themselves, but they seem friendly about it all. I pray that they choose Oregon. I pray that Bobbi will get over being mad at me.

Night

There's a doctor here. Mrs. Hull had him look at Me Too. The doctor thinks he'll live. But he must ride in the wagon now and not walk. He also can't talk. He just mumbles. It's done something awful to his tongue.

I know I should feel bad. But I don't. He's as mean with his mouth as Mrs. Meaney.

August 6

I'm so happy! Bobbi's family is staying on the north trail with us. All their wagons chose to stick together. There will be lots of Druckers in Oregon.

I hope they'll settle near us.

I hope Bobbi will talk to me soon.

August 11

I haven't written about Grampa much. Because I don't see him often! He's dropped back and spends his days with the sisters.

Then tonight, he suddenly appeared. He sat down to supper with Ma and Pa and me. He acted like he hadn't been gone a week. He was kind to old Mrs. Meaney. For the first time ever, I saw her smile.

She has no teeth.

Afterward, Grampa even helped Ma store the plates and cooking things. When it was time to bed down, Grampa got his bedding and laid it next to mine.

I waited for him to say something. But in minutes, he was snoring, while I lay awake. I wonder what he's planning.

August 12

Tonight Becky began fussing. Aunt Lizzie picked her up. Suddenly Becky said, "Where's Rachel?"

It's the first time she's asked for Rachel.

Aunt Lizzie pointed at a heron flying over. "Look. A big bird!" she said.

Becky said, "Rachel!"

Aunt Lizzie handed me Becky, then ducked behind her wagon.

I put Becky on my shoulders. "Want a horsy ride?" I said.

"I want Rachel," she said. "Where'd she go?"

My throat got tight. I said, "I don't know where she went."

That is the truth.

August 14

Grampa's been riding beside us for three whole days. He doesn't say much. It's like he has a secret. I keep waiting for him to tell me. I think I know what it is. I don't mind. Grandma's been dead a long time, and he's lonesome.

But I wonder what Ma will say.

August 15

Mrs. Gibbons seems to have gotten smaller. She barely speaks. Mrs. Hull has taken to riding with her and the little ones.

Before supper

Tonight, when we made camp, we heard shouting. It was coming from the Wests' wagon. Everyone stopped to listen. People say Mr. West beats his wife.

Ma told me to go on about my business. I tried to, but I couldn't help but hear. Mr. West was shouting that his wife spends all day looking around and daydreaming.

I think everyone was embarrassed. All but old Mrs. Meaney. She dropped her knitting and leaned forward in her chair — in *Ma's* chair. She seemed to enjoy every mean word.

Snake River

A terrible crossing. A treacherous crossing. My heart is still thumping bad tonight. We had to cross a roaring river. The men chained the wagons together, one behind the other. Then teams of oxen were chained together to help pull. Like other times, horsemen rode alongside. They whipped and shouted at the oxen.

Oh, but first, we had to make the wagons more watertight. We used bedding and sheets soaked in tar. We even used our clothing.

We made it across. I stayed in the wagon with little Becky. Pa said I must.

I was relieved. But now I'm sure that Pa knows that I'm scared.

August, hot, hot, hot

One of the hardest days yet. The sun was scorching. My arms are sunburned bad, even though Ma covers them with grease. Then, in the midst of this blue sky, a storm broke. The sky turned blacker than night. The wind whipped up. The horses tucked their tails under themselves. The oxen quivered. The wagon covers billowed. And then the rain came down. And ice. Hail. It was so wicked, we stopped. We took shelter as best we could.

For an hour it raged. I've never seen a storm like it. In Missouri we don't have storms like this.

Grampa and I huddled under the wagon. I didn't see Pa. But Ma was inside the wagon with Becky. I picked up a chunk of ice as big as a rock and held it in my hands. I don't know why. I just did. I held it a long time. I wanted to see how long I could stand the pain. Tears came. But I held on to it.

After a minute, Grampa reached over and took my hand. He made me drop the ice chunk. But I couldn't stop the tears. Grampa just held my hand. He held it for a long, long time.

He said softly, "Don't fret. The end is in sight."

I didn't answer. But inside my head, thoughts ran around like little mice: Mr. Allison is dead, Mr. Gibbons got killed, Mr. West is vicious, and poor little babies are dead. My feet hurt. I'm hot. I'm cold. I'm scared of water. I'm scared of Indians. Practically every day I'm scared half to death. Bobbi is mad at me. And I don't know why I care.

Grampa murmured, "I know, I know." As if he were listening in on my thoughts.

I feel sad and horrid inside.

Late August

Nights are cooler now. We find it easier to sleep. But Cousin Daniel says cold nights mean early winter. He's pushing us hard to make even more miles each day. Yet, in the mountains, it's harder to move our wagons. It's also harder to walk. We go single file. It's especially hard walking because my shoes are worn out. Pa fixed them with strips of leather, but they flap and trip me.

I reread this diary. All I do is complain. I should be more like Ma or Adam. Ma didn't want to go. But now she makes the best of it. And Adam is quiet and he prays.

August 24

Tonight, when we camped, I looked close at Aunt Lizzie. She looks different. She's fat.

And then I was happy because I realized —
there will be a new baby in the family!

August 25

Soon we'll be at Fort Boise. And then,
instantly, we'll be in Oregon. But even after we
get to Oregon, we're not to the valley yet. We
still have a long way to go.

It is very cold at night. And funny, one
would think it would ease tempers. It doesn't.
Men are beginning to fight. Women are
tight-lipped. The children whine and cry.

Cousin Daniel says hurry on. Or, he says, "I
will go on without you." You can see he means
it. Today, Mr. West got really mad. He wanted
to stop and rest. Pa had to tell him to grow up.

September 1

Tonight a fight broke out. We were making camp. The oxen had been taken off their yokes. Suddenly Mr. West began whipping the oxen about their heads. He whipped and whipped them.

Mrs. West started to scream. Mr. West turned the whip handle around. He was going after Mrs. West with it. Pa ran and grabbed for Mr. West. But Mr. West took the handle and cracked Pa in the head.

Suddenly Mrs. West jumped down from the wagon. She had a fry pan in her hand. She bounced it off Mr. West's head, and he dropped right down in the dust.

I only wish she had struck him long ago.

Ma bandaged up Pa's head. It's cut but not deep.

Pa says it's a good thing we're almost there. Tempers won't last much longer.

In the Cascades

Today, something terrible. And wonderful. We were high in the Cascade Mountains. Partway up, we had to ford another stream. It was swift and deep. Ma was in the front of our wagon with Becky on her lap. Pa was on the far side in the water. I was in the water on the other side. Suddenly our wagon began to tip.

Pa pushed. Ma shouted, "Lean this way!" She shoved herself hard against the side of the wagon. I looked up at her and as I looked, Becky tumbled from her lap. She fell into the raging river, almost by my feet.

Before I could grab her, she was swept downstream.

I dove after her. I don't know what I was thinking. Nothing.

She disappeared under the water.

I dove under, too.

I was swimming. But I don't know how to swim. Under the water, I saw her dress. A bit of white, floating. I reached for it. I got it and pulled it to me. It was heavy — she was heavy. I held her to me. I lifted her up and I struggled to shore.

People were shouting. I could hear them. Becky's face was white. And blue. She didn't make a sound. I shook her hard. I shook her again. "Wake up!" I yelled.

She coughed. She spit water. And then she began to wail. She howled.

I blinked back tears and hugged her tight.

People crowded around. Someone took her from me. They handed her to Ma.

My baby sister is alive tonight.

Ma and Pa just hug me and hug me and hug me.

Later

Pa told me I was very brave. I told him I was scared stiff. Pa said that's what courage is all about.

Still later

I was sitting alone by the fire. Bobbi came and sat beside me.

I wondered what she was up to. But I was too tired to care. All I could think of was Becky.

After a long while, Bobbi said, "You mad at me?"

"No."

"You should be," she said. "I was a ninny."

I looked at her.

"I was wrong," she said. "About you being a chicken."

"Oh," I said. I could feel myself blushing. I looked down at the embers. "I don't know," I said. "I was scared stiff."

"Yeah," she said. "I'm scared, too."

"Of what?"

She waved her hand around. "This. I'm tired. And scared. Do you think we'll ever get there?"

I nodded. "I think so," I said. "I think we will."

Cascades still

Up and up and over the Cascades. Soon we'll be where we set out to be. Pa did a count. He said about one of every fifteen people who started out have died. And we've lost more oxen and cows and mules than you can shake a stick at. But we're almost there.

Home, Pa says.

Home? We left our home behind.

Mid-September

When we make camp, we're too tired to even talk. People just eat, then bed down. Mrs. Hull is like a mother hen to Mrs. Gibbons. She fusses round. It's like she has adopted all three of them — January and February and Mrs. Gibbons, too.

I think Mrs. Hull has a very big heart.

Mr. West seems better behaved. But Ma says Mrs. West should sleep with that fry pan by her side from now on.

A cold night and raining

Last night when we stopped, we didn't unyoke the oxen. We were sure they'd run away. They're yearning for food and water and rest. So we let them sleep in the yokes. But this morning, two were dead.

Dead? But they've come so far with us. Ma promises it will be better when we get to the valley.

I wonder how she can be so sure.

Next day

I was gathering firewood by the stream when Grampa came to me. Miss Emmaline was with him. He said, "I'm married, Josh boy."

Just like that!

"Reverend Jackson did the honors last night," he said. "This here's my bride."

I just stared. And then I said, "Oh." Or something else just as brilliant.

Miss Emmaline blushed.

"Tell your ma," he said.

"Me?" I said.

Grampa nodded and grinned. He said, "I don't have your kind of courage, son."

Later

I told Ma about Grampa.

She pulled her mouth into a tight line. "No fool like an old fool," she said.

Pa just winked at me.

September 27

I'm so happy to have Charlie and Adam and Bobbi walking with me again. And even Me Too. He's maybe not so bad as he used to be. Things aren't so bad when you have friends.

October

We're almost there. Pa says another day, maybe two. The end of the trail. We're so weary. The oxen are more weary. So everyone walks now, even the babies. Aunt Lizzie is getting big with child. But she walks, too. Only Mrs. Meaney rides. And knits. And complains.

But poor Buster! The pads on his paws refuse to heal. So Bobbi and Charlie and Adam and I take turns carrying him. Charlie is nice to Bobbi now. I don't know why, but it makes me happy. It's bad when your friends don't like one another.

Nighttime

We are over the Cascades. We've come to the valley. We feel the moisture in the air. It's so different from the plains.

I think I should be happy. I am happy. We are where we set out to be. But I'm so tired.

Morning

This morning we looked around us. We seem to be on top of the world. The wind blows and the leaves dance. It's so different from St. Joseph. It's green, even now in October.

Ma held Becky in her arms. She has hardly put Becky down since the river accident. She pointed out at the valley and said, "Well, what about that, Mr. McCullough?"

"I think we made it, Mrs. McCullough," Pa answered.

Then he turned and reached for me. "We made it, Josh," he said.

I nodded. "We did," I said.

Later still

Soon we'll each choose and mark off our square mile of land. But for now, we set up tents. We all want to stop living in wagons. Aunt Lizzie and Uncle Arthur put their tent right beside our own. Bobbi's family put their tent on the other side.

And then, it made me mad to see — but the Meaneys took a place close by. Old Mrs. Meaney is still as mean as she can be. I don't think the mountain air has changed her mood at all.

Grampa set his tent a long way off. The Hulls and the three Gibbonses have made a place together. I'm glad that they care for one another. And to think — I had hated Frederick Hull.

So we have a little neighborhood, just like back at the beginning of the trail.

Next day

Grampa came to our tent with Miss Emmaline. Is that what I should call her? I know I can't call her Grandma!

Ma was inside, sweeping. She turned and saw them in the tent doorway. She quick brushed her hair out of her eyes.

She looked at Miss Emmaline. She looked at her pa. No one spoke.

And then — oh, I am so proud of Ma!

She went right up to Miss Emmaline. She kissed her on the cheek. Not just one cheek. But two.

Later

I can hardly believe this: At supper time, Mrs. Meaney hobbled over to Ma. She handed Ma an armful of something blue and fluffy — that thing she has been knitting the whole journey long.

"Here!" she said, real grufflike. "A blanket. You're a good enough woman."

And then she hobbled away.

Ma just stood there. I believe she was stunned. After a minute, she stammered, "Thank you."

A good enough woman? I hardly know what to make of it.

Early morning, October 12

This morning, Pa picked up a paintbrush and a bucket of tar. He said he'd been thinking what to write on our wagon. He looked at Ma.

"Well?" he said.

Ma smiled. "Go ahead," she said.

"What?" he said.

"You know," she said.

Pa just looked at her a minute. And then, kind of quiet-like, he said, "Home?"

Ma nodded. "Home," she said.

Pa looked at me then, his eyebrows up.

I thought for a minute. Home? Was it home? It was — strange. I looked around me. There was Becky. And Ma. And Pa. And Grampa and even Miss Emmaline. And Aunt Lizzie and Uncle Arthur and Charlie and Bobbi and — and everybody.

I smiled. I took a deep breath, and nodded.

Pa turned back to the wagon.

And he painted across the back: *Home. We*
are home.

I do think those are the best words ever.

Historical Note

In the mid-1800s in the United States, there was a huge migration of folks leaving their homes in the East and surging westward. They went in covered wagons. They went by foot. They went on horseback and muleback.

Independence, Missouri, a starting point for the Oregon Trail.

There were sometimes up to 70 wagons in a wagon train.

They went in huge caravans with many others for company. And some brave souls traveled with no more than two or three others. But go they did.

They went for many different reasons. Some were in search of a better life, for they were promised land in Oregon, free land. Some went because times in the East were hard, with a drought, worn-out farmland, and a depression. Some went to escape the terrible plague of disease that was ravaging the country at the time. And some went just

Fording a river.

because they were restless, for the spirit of adventure was strong in early Americans. These early settlers who went to Oregon and California were called emigrants at first — for it was felt that they were migrating to a foreign land. And, indeed, they were. Both the United States and Great Britain had laid claim to that land, and it had not yet become a part of the United States. Once it was annexed, however, the dreams became a reality — lush land, and free land.

But the cost was high in other ways than money. Some did not live to see this promised land, for the trail across the lonesome prairie was fraught with danger. There were the struggles with heat, fierce sun, prairie fires, winds, and vicious ice and hailstorms, the likes of which many had never seen in the East.

There were snakes and wolves to contend with. There were drowning accidents and accidents when wagons overturned, sometimes killing the occupants. There were

There were many deaths on the Oregon Trail. This gravestone marked one person's burial site.

also other natural disasters, such as illness. Though many settlers went on the trail to escape disease, in fact, they brought it with them. Many died and were buried right

Wagons on the Oregon Trail formed a corral at night for safety.

The pioneers hunted game for fresh meat on the trail.

on the trail. There was also the constant threat of Indian attack, for the Indians believed that no one owned the land, and the settlers believed otherwise.

Yet for the fortunate ones who did make it, the trail and the trials brought them to a promised land. They had found what they had come looking for — land and opportunity and, for some, simply a fresh start. They were the first to truly succeed in expanding our country "from sea to shining sea."

About the Author

Patricia Hermes has never crossed the prairie in a covered wagon, but she has had much experience with the costs of uprooting a family and moving from one part of the country to another. When she wrote about Joshua, she relied at least a bit on the experience of the boys she knows so well — her four sons.

She says, "Today, though we are spared the trials of the early settlers, there is still the deep loneliness and loss that one feels when leaving behind one's home and family and friends. And some family is just too dear to leave behind. That is why, in writing this book, I could not bear for Joshua to leave his grampa behind. So Grampa came with him. In the end, Joshua was able finally to overcome all the hardships of the move. And when settled in his new land, he began to feel at home — as have we."

Patricia Hermes is the author of more than thirty books for children and young adults. She has written another book in the My America series, *Our Strange New Land*, the story of Elizabeth Barker in Jamestown, Virginia, in 1609. Many of her books have received awards, from Children's Choice awards to state awards, ALA Best Books, and ALA Notable Book awards.

Acknowledgments

Grateful acknowledgment is made for permission to reprint the following:

Cover portrait and frontispiece by Glenn Harrington.

Page 101: Oregon Trail, Independence, Missouri, Oregon Historical Society, Neg. #ORH5220 #838.

Page 102: View of Chimney Rock region: drawing by William Henry Jackson, 1929, The Granger Collection, New York, New York.

Page 103: "Stuck Fast" from Hutchings Panoramic Scenes, crossing the Plains; Hutchings Illustrated California Magazine, Oregon Historical Society, Neg. #39601 OPS.

Page 104 (top): Gravestone, The Kansas State Historical Society, Neg. #TEO #36, Topeka, Kansas.

Page 104 (bottom): Transportation of Army supplies to Utah — yoking cattle, 1859, Corbis-Bettman.

Page 105: Life on the Frontier, New York Public Library Picture Collection.

Other books in the My America series

For Samuel James Hermes

Copyright © 2001 by Patricia Hermes

Library of Congress Cataloging-in-Publication Data
Hermes, Patricia.
Westward to Home: Joshua's Diary / by Patricia Hermes.
p. cm. – (My America)
Summary: In 1848, nine-year-old Joshua Martin McCullough writes a journal of his family's journey from Missouri to Oregon in a covered wagon.
Includes a historical note about westward migration.
ISBN 0-439-11209-5; ISBN 0-439-38899-6 (pbk.)
[1. Overland journeys to the Pacific—Fiction. 2. Frontier and pioneer life—West (U.S.)—Fiction. 3. West (U.S.)—Fiction. 4. Diaries—Fiction.] I. Title. II. Series.
PZ7.H4317 We 2001
[Fic]—dc21 00-044666

10 9 8 7 6 5 4 3 2 1   02 03 04 05

The display type was set in Cooper Old Style
The text type was set in Goudy
Book design by Elizabeth B. Parisi
Photo research by Zoe Moffitt

Printed in the U.S.A. 23
First paperback edition, August 2002